Dear Parents,

Welcome to the Scholastic Reader series. We have taken over 80 years of experience with teachers, parents, and children and put it into a program that is designed to match your child's interests and skills.

Level 1—Short sentences and stories made up of words kids can sound out using their phonics skills and words that are important to remember.

Level 2—Longer sentences and stories with words kids need to know and new "big" words that they will want to know.

Level 3—From sentences to paragraphs to longer stories, these books have large "chunks" of texts and are made up of a rich vocabulary.

Level 4—First chapter books with more words and fewer pictures.

It is important that children learn to read well enough to succeed in school and beyond. Here are ideas for reading this book with your child:

- Look at the book together. Encourage your child to read the title and make a prediction about the story.
- Read the book together. Encourage your child to sound out words when appropriate. When your child struggles, you can help by providing the word.
- Encourage your child to retell the story. This is a great way to check for comprehension.
- Have your child take the fluency test on the last page to check progress.

Scholastic Readers are designed to support your child's efforts to learn how to read at every age and every stage. Enjoy helping your child learn to read and love to read.

　　　　　—**Francie Alexander**
　　　　　　Chief Education Officer
　　　　　　Scholastic Education

SUPERTWINS ™
AND THE SNEAKY, SLIMY BOOK WORMS

BY **B.J. JAMES**
ILLUSTRATED BY **CHRIS DEMAREST**

For Kendra
—B.J.J.

To my own caped crusader, Ethan.
—C.D.

Text copyright © 2004 by Brian Masino.
Illustrations copyright © 2004 by Chris Demarest.
All rights reserved. Published by Scholastic Inc.
SCHOLASTIC, CARTWHEEL BOOKS, and associated logos are trademarks and/or registered trademarks of Scholastic Inc.

Library of Congress Cataloging-in-Publication Data
James, Brian.
  Supertwins and the sneaky, slimy book worms / by B. J. James; illustrated by Chris Demarest.
    p. cm. — (Scholastic readers. Level 2) "Cartwheel Books."
Summary: Superhero twins Timmy and Tammy hide in their school to look for the thieves responsible for stealing all the books.
  ISBN 0-439-46626-1
  [1. Heroes—Fiction. 2. Twins—Fiction. 3. Brothers and sisters—Fiction. 4. Worms—Fiction. 5. Schools—Fiction.] I. Demarest, Chris L., ill. II. Title. III. Series.
PZ7.J153585 St 2004
[E]—dc21
2003007800

10 9 8 7 6 5 4 3 2   04 05 06 07 08
              Printed in the U.S.A. 24 • First printing, February 2004

Scholastic Reader — Level 2

SCHOLASTIC INC.

New York   Toronto   London   Auckland   Sydney
Mexico City   New Delhi   Hong Kong   Buenos Aires

Chapter 1

Tabby and I have a
super nice teacher.
Her name is Mrs. Shelly.

But one day,
Mrs. Shelly was really mad.
All the books were gone!

"Class, this is not funny," Mrs. Shelly said.
"Who took the books?"

Someone was behind this!
I was sure about that.

"Who do you think stole the books?"
I asked Tabby.

"I think it was Dan," Tabby said.
Dan is my friend.
Tabby does not like Dan.
"No it wasn't!" I told her.
"You take that back!"

Tabby made a face at me.

Sometimes having a twin sister
is worse than having homework!

Another teacher, Ms. Ellen, came into our class

She said the books in her room were gone, too
ALL the books in the whole school were gone.
Ms. Ellen had a note in her hand.

She read it to us.

We took your books. We are getting them cleaned. Sincerely The Bookworms

"That is very nice of them," Mrs. Shelly said.

The principal made an announcement.
He was closing the school.
"School will open again when the books are back," the principal said.

All the kids got to go home.

Chapter 2

Tabby and I hid under our desks.
Soon, the school was empty.
Those Slimy Book Worms couldn't be far.

I knew worms lived underground.
The basement was underground.
Maybe the Book Worms were in the baseme

IN THE BASEMENT...

the Slimy Book Worms were cheering.
All of the books were there.
The books were covered with slime.
YUCKY!

Tabby and I snuck in.
"We have to stop them!" Tabby said.

I had a plan.
We learned all about worms in school.
Worms don't like heat.
We could use our super powers to warm things u

Tabby raised her hands.

She shut her eyes.
Then sunbeams shot
from her hands.

BLAM!

The basement was bright and sunny.

It was getting super warm.
Those Slimy Book Worms started to sweat.
They didn't know what was happening.

I jumped out from our hiding place.

"Game over!" I shouted.
"We are taking our books back!"

Tabby kept making it hotter.
I kept running around.
The Slimy Book Worms kept chasing me.
They were getting tired.
It was too hot for them.

The worms were shrinking.
This heat thing was really working.

Soon, I was out of breath.
I had to stop running.
Even superheroes get tired.

I looked around.
I didn't see any worms.
I did see Tabby.
She was standing next to me.

Where did they go?" I asked.
They are right there, silly," Tabby answered.

The worms had shrunk back to normal size!
Good work!" I told Tabby.
Good work, yourself!" she said.

Tabby got a small jar.
She picked up a worm and put it in.
The worms were super slimy.
"GROSS!" Tabby said.

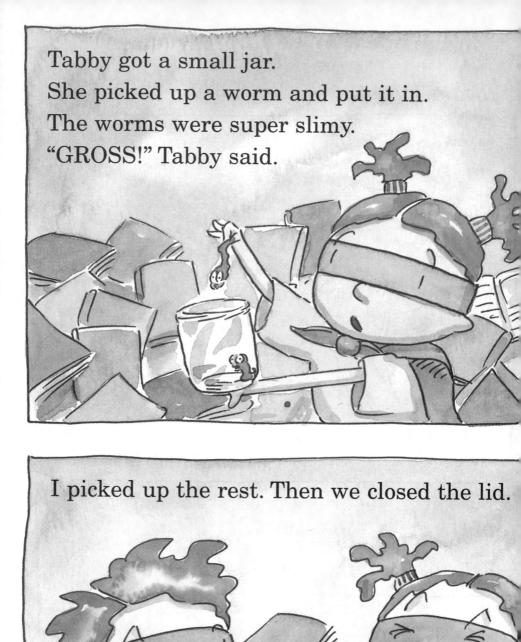

I picked up the rest. Then we closed the lid.

Chapter 3

"We have to put these books back," Tabby said.

Tabby zoomed down the hall.
She wasn't looking.
"Slow down!" I told her.
She didn't listen.

Then . . . CRASH!

Tabby flew right into the principal!

"You kids shouldn't be running," he said.
"I'm sorry," Tabby said.

"Are those OUR books?" he asked.

We nodded.
We were afraid he had learned our secret.

"But those books aren't even CLEAN!"
the principal said. "The note said
you would clean them. I want you to
clean them right now!"

Our secret was safe, but...
superheroes have to do ALL the work!

Fluency Fun

The words in each list below end in the same sounds.
Read the words in a list.
Read them again.
Read them faster.
Try to read all 15 words in one minute.

dirty	room	book
funny	zoom	cook
really	broom	took
sorry	groom	cookbook
sunny	mushroom	notebook

Look for these words in the story.

principal   whole   everything

gone   around